Fantastic Fairy Tales

HANSEL AND GRETEL

An imprint of Om Books International

There once lived a poor woodcutter who had two children - a boy named Hansel and a little girl named Gretel. Sadly, they had a stepmother who didn't love them at all.

The family was very poor. One day, the stepmother said to the father, "There is no food on the table! Do you want me to die? We must leave the children in the woods to fend for themselves." The poor woodcutter could say nothing.

But Hansel heard everything and quickly picked up some round, white pebbles from the yard.

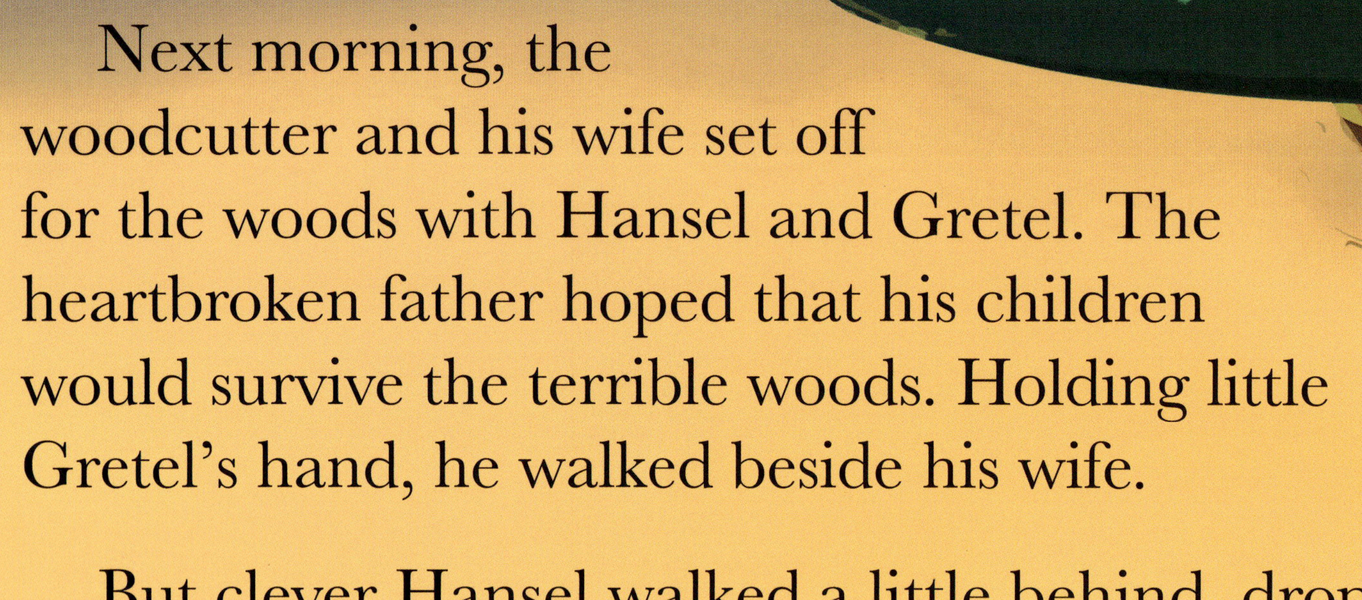

Next morning, the woodcutter and his wife set off for the woods with Hansel and Gretel. The heartbroken father hoped that his children would survive the terrible woods. Holding little Gretel's hand, he walked beside his wife.

But clever Hansel walked a little behind, dropping the round, white pebbles all along the path.

When the parents left them and went away, Hansel and Gretel just followed the pebbles right back to their cottage!

The woodcutter was relieved to find his children back home, safe and sound. He hugged them close to his heart, thinking all would be well now.

But that was not to be. The cruel stepmother kept grumbling all through dinner and made the woodcutter promise that the children would go.

This time, Hansel couldn't go into the yard for the pebbles, so he hid a chunk of bread in his pocket instead.

Next day, Hansel dropped little bits of bread all along the path. What he didn't realise was that the birds were eating the bread as soon as he dropped it!

That evening, when the children tried to find their way home, there were no bread bits to guide them.

Hopelessly lost and scared, Hansel and Gretel spent a dark, dreary night in the deep woods.

"Whoo, whoo, whoo!" Strange sounds frightened little Gretel and she held on to her brother.

"Don't worry, sweet Gretel," Hansel said to her, "we'll definitely find our way back in the morning."

When Hansel and Gretel woke up next morning, they saw a strange little cottage right in front of their eyes. It seemed the cottage was a giant cake!

And indeed, it was a giant chocolate cake! The walls were studded with candies and lollipops stood for chimneys. The windowpanes were made of frosting and doughnut flowers grew all around.

There was licorice and lemon drops, chocolate bits and maple syrup! The children broke off bits and began to eat hungrily.

"Aha!" exclaimed an old woman, coming to the door, taking the children by surprise. "Oh do come inside, precious little ones! There are delicious pancakes for you inside, and gingerbread too."

Soon, Hansel and Gretel were seated at the old woman's table, eating the best meal of their lives. They were so happy to have found the cottage and thought the old lady to be very kind.

But the old lady was really a terrible, wicked witch! She used to tempt little children with her magic cottage, then she would fatten them up and cook them.

"Hee-hee-hee," she cackled as the children slept. "This boy will make a delicious meal when he's all fattened up!"

The witch threw poor Hansel into a cage and stuffed him with all kinds of food day and night for many days.

Little Gretel was made to scrub floors and do all the household chores without a minute's rest.

Then, one day, the witch decided it was time to make a meal of Hansel.

"Bring me the turnips and the carrots, you lazy girl!" she screamed at Gretel, stirring a cauldron of broth. "Baked Hansel will be delicious with some hot turnip broth!"

Poor Gretel didn't want her dear brother to die, and she was desperately trying to find some way to save him. Just then, she saw the old witch open the oven door and lean in to see if it was hot enough.

Gretel ran up to the witch quickly and with a mighty push on the witch's behind, Gretel sent the old hag screaming into the oven fires to be burnt to cinders.

Then, little Gretel freed her brother from the cage and took him to a room full of treasure. She had found the room while cleaning the cottage one day.

"Let's take all this home, dear Hansel," she said. "Then we can live happily with Father in our cottage."

Hansel found the witch's horse-cart behind the cottage. It was a magical cart with a magical horse. The horse neighed once and all the treasure loaded in the cart! He neighed again and galloped away to the children's cottage outside the woods, while the witch's magic cottage fell to pieces.

The woodcutter had thrown out his cruel wife and had told her never to return. He was sitting glumly outside his cottage when he looked up and saw his children running towards him!

And so the small family was united and they all lived happily with their very own magic horse-cart and all the riches in the world.